# COME UNTO ME

## AN OVERVIEW OF THE BIBLE IN POETRY FOR CHILDREN

BERNICE JACKSON GRAHAM

*Come Unto Me*
by Bernice Jackson Graham

Printed in the United States of America

Library of Congress Control Number: 2002116118
ISBN 1-591603-65-X



Xulon Press
10640 Main Street
Suite 204
Fairfax, VA 22030
(703) 934-4411
XulonPress.com

To order additional copies, call 1-866-909-BOOK (2665).

To Mark & Brenda
May God Bless
You!
Love
6-22-03

# DEDICATION

This book is dedicated to my firstborn grandson,

Julian Alexander Graham.

His zest for learning inspires, challenges,

and encourages me.

# *TABLE OF CONTENTS*

# *INTRODUCTION*

*__COME UNTO ME__ was written to give children an easy way to learn about the information presented in the __Bible.__*

*The key verses quoted at the end of each poem will help the child to memorize verses in relationship to the stories in the __Bible__, and to better understand the Word of God.*

*This book is also intended to give just enough information to encourage the child to ask questions about the events mentioned in __COME UNTO ME.__*

Jesus said, "Let the little children
***COME UNTO ME,*** and do not hinder them,
for the kingdom of heaven belongs
to such as these."

Matthew 19:14

## *BOOKS OF THE OLD TESTAMENT*

| | | |
|---|---|---|
| *Genesis* | *2 Chonicles* | *Daniel* |
| *Exodus* | *Ezra* | *Hosea* |
| *Leviticus* | *Nehemiah* | *Joel* |
| *Numbers* | *Esther* | *Amos* |
| *Deuteronomy* | *Job* | *Obadiah* |
| *Joshua* | *Psalms* | *Jonah* |
| *Judges* | *Proverbs* | *Micah* |
| *Ruth* | *Ecclesiastes* | *Nahum* |
| *1 Samuel* | *Song of Solomon* | *Habakkuk* |
| *2 Samuel* | *Isaiah* | *Zephaniah* |
| *1 Kings* | *Jeremiah* | *Haggai* |
| *2 Kings* | *Lamentations* | *Zechariah* |
| *1 Chronicles* | *Ezekiel* | *Malachi* |

# *INTRODUCTION TO THE OLD TESTAMENT*

***The Old Testament, the first part of the Holy Scriptures, contains 39 books. It tells of the covenant between God and His people. It contains a record of their history to show how faithfully they observed this covenant.***

***For more than two thousand years, millions of people from all over the world have turned to the Old Testament for guidance and answers to life's problems. We believe that the Old Testament is the word of God.***

# *GENESIS*

***Genesis is the book of beginnings.***
***God created Adam and Eve.***
***He made the plants and animals,***
***And the serpent who came to deceive.***

***"In the beginning, God created the heavens and the earth."***

***1:1***

# *EXODUS*

***Exodus tells about Moses,***
***And the struggling Israelites.***
***God delivered them from Egypt,***
***And helped them in their flight.***

***"The Lord will fight for you; you need only be still."***

***14:14***

# *LEVITICUS*

***Leviticus teaches us how***
***To get right with God above.***
***It tells of all the offerings***
***The people gave to show their love.***

***"I am the Lord your God, consecrate yourselves and be holy, because I am holy.***

***11:44***

# ***NUMBERS***

***The book of Numbers tells the story***
***Of God's people in the wilderness.***
***They complained about the manna,***
***And they doubted if God would bless.***

***"The Lord is slow to anger, abounding in love and forgiving sin and rebellion."***

***14:18***

# *DEUTERONOMY*

***The Ten Commandments is the law***
***God sent to us from above.***
***They tell us not to lie or steal,***
***But to show respect and love.***

***"Love the Lord your God with all your heart, and with all your soul, and with all your strength."***

***6:5***

# *JOSHUA*

***Joshua lead the Israelites***
***Into the Promised Land.***
***He defeated all their enemies***
***As he held to God's strong hand.***

***"Be strong and courageous. Do not be terrified; do not be discouraged, for the Lord your God will be with you wherever you go."***

***1:9***

# ***JUDGES***

***In Judges we meet the twelve leaders,***
***Who God raised up to save the Nation,***
***Because the people disobeyed their God,***
***And gave in to all temptation.***

***"In those days there were no king in Israel, but every man did that which was right in his own eyes."***

***17:6***

# ***RUTH***

***Ruth loved Naomi, her mother-in-law.***
***She stayed with her throughout their grief.***
***Ruth followed her back to Bethlehem,***
***And met Boaz, who provided relief.***

***"But Ruth replied…Where you go, I will go, and where you stay, I will stay. Your people will be my people, and your God, my God.***

***1:16***

# *1 SAMUEL*

***God blessed Hannah with Samuel,***
***And God was with him as he grew.***
***Samuel named Saul as Israel's king,***
***But to God Saul was not true.***

***"Does the Lord delight in burnt offerings and sacrifices as much as in obeying the voice of the Lord? To obey is better than sacrifice…"***

***15:22***

# *2 SAMUEL*

***David became the king of Israel.***
***He was a man after God's own heart.***
***His love for Bathsheba caused him to sin,***
***But from David God did not depart.***

***"You are my lamp, O Lord; the Lord turns my darkness into light."***

***22:29***

# *1 KINGS*

***In 1 Kings we meet Solomon.***
***David appointed him as king.***
***Solomon asked God for wisdom.***
***It's worth more than everything.***

***"And if you walk in my ways, and obey my statues and commands as David did, I will give you a long life."***

***3:14***

# *2 KINGS*

***Second Kings is the history***
***Of the great kings of Israel.***
***Some ruled in a godly manner,***
***But others didn't do so well.***

***"...He did much evil in the eyes of the Lord, provoking Him to anger."***

***21:6***

# *1 Chronicles*

***1 Chronicles begins with Adam,***
***Followed by a list of all his kin.***
***God called each one by his name,***
***And their love He hoped to win.***

***"Ascribe to the Lord, O families of nations, ascribe to the Lord glory and strength, ascribe to the Lord the glory due His name..."***

***16:28-29***

# *2 CHRONICLES*

***Because God gave Solomon wisdom,***
***He ruled his people well.***
***But after King Solomon's death,***
***Into sin both nations fell.***

***"…for the Lord your God is gracious and compassionate. He will not turn His face from you, if you return to Him."***

***30:9***

# *EZRA*

***In Ezra God kept His promise***
***When He returned the Jews to their land.***
***Then they rebuilt His holy temple,***
***And were protected by His hand.***

***"...The gracious hand of our God is on everyone who looks to Him, but His great anger is against all who forsake Him."***

***8:22***

# ***NEHEMIAH***

***Nehemiah rebuilt Jerusalem's walls,***
***And the Israelites confessed their sin.***
***Ezra boldly read from the Book of The Law,***
***And they let the joy of the Lord come in.***

***"...This day is sacred to our Lord. Do not grieve, for the joy of the Lord is your strength."***

***8:10***

# ***ESTHER***

***Esther became the queen of Persia,***
***When Queen Vashti angered the King.***
***Because of her loyalty to Mordecai,***
***The Jews escaped much suffering.***

***"...and who knows but that you have come to royal position for such a time as this."***

***4:14***

# ***JOB***

***Job was God's faithful servant***
***Who the devil tried to destroy.***
***He stole his health, wealth, and family,***
***But God graciously restored his joy.***

***"He does not take His eyes off the righteous: He enthrones them with kings and exalts them forever."***

***36:7***

# *PSALMS*

***We read the prayers of David,***
***Whose life was filled with strife.***
***By faith he wrote hymns of praises***
***To God who protected his life.***

***"My mouth will speak in praise of the Lord. Let every creature praise His holy name forever and ever."***

***145:21***

# ***PROVERBS***

***Proverbs teach the laws for living,***
***And how to treat our fellow man.***
***If we follow all these teachings,***
***We gain favor at God's hand.***

***"Listen to advice and accept instruction, and in the end you will be wise."***

***19:20***

# *ECCLESIASTES*

***Ecclesiastes is full of wisdom***
***To teach us the lessons of life.***
***We seek pleasure in all the wrong things,***
***That's why our days are filled with strife.***

***"Fear God and keep His commandments, for this is the whole duty of man."***

***12:13***

# *SONG OF SOLOMON*

***Solomon, a great king of Israel,***
***Disguised himself as a shepherd boy,***
***Fell in love with a beautiful maiden,***
***And together they discovered true joy.***

***"Many waters cannot quench love; rivers cannot wash it away. If one were to give all the wealth of his house for love, it would be utterly scorned."***

***8:7***

# *ISAIAH*

***Isaiah warns the people of Judah***
***That God is angry about their sinning.***
***He promises them that if they repent,***
***God will give them a new beginning.***

***"I will praise You, O Lord, although You were angry with me, Your anger has turned away, and You have comforted me.***

***12:1***

# ***JEREMIAH***

***The people of Judah were unholy.***
***Jeremiah begged them to repent.***
***They beat him and threw him into a well.***
***Then Babylon destroyed their government.***

***"This is what the Lord Almighty, the God of Israel says, Reform your ways and your actions, and I will let you live in this place."***

***7:3***

# *LAMENTATIONS*

***Lamentations is about the Daughters of Zion,***
***And how God punished them for their sin.***
***It tells of death, heartbreak and sorrow,***
***And of God's forgiveness they begged to win.***

***"Let us examine our ways and test them, and let us return to the Lord.***

***3:40***

# ***EZEKIEL***

***Ezekiel gives us a picture***
***Of God's wrath when His people sin.***
***Being merciful He gave back their land,***
***And they built God's temple within.***

***"Then the people of Israel will no longer stray from me, nor will they defile themselves anymore with their sins. They will be my people, and I will be their God, declares the Sovereign Lord."***

***14:11***

# *DANIEL*

***Daniel and his friends remained true to God,***
***Even in the furnace and the lions' den.***
***They refused to bow before other gods,***
***That's why God protected them from evil men.***

***"...Praise be to the God of Shadrack, Meshack, and Abednego, who has sent His angel and rescued His servants..."***

***3:28***

# HOSEA

***God was angry with the people of Israel.***
***They made idol gods and continued to sin.***
***But He being a God of compassion and love,***
***Gave them a chance to serve Him again.***

***"But I am the Lord your God, who brought you out of Egypt. You shall acknowledge no God but me, no Savior but me."***

***13:4***

# ***JOEL***

***Joel preached to the people of Judah,***
***After the locust attacked the city.***
***He begged them to repent and return to God,***
***And asked God to show them pity.***

***"…Return to the Lord, for He is gracious and compassionate, slow to anger, and abounding in love."***

***2:13***

# *AMOS*

***God spoke to Amos, His prophet.***
***His message was loud and clear.***
***He was going to punish His people,***
***Because they sinned and had no fear.***

***"Seek good, not evil, that you may live. Then the Lord God Almighty will be with you as you say He is."***

***5:14***

# ***OBADIAH***

***The smallest book of the Old Testament,***
***Yet, its lesson is great as can be:***
***God teaches us to love our brother,***
***In a vision He allowed Obadiah to see.***

***"You should not look down on your brother in the day of his misfortune…nor boast so much in the day of their trouble."***

***2:12***

# *JONAH*

***God gave Jonah an order;***
***To Nineveh he must go.***
***But Jonah ran the other way,***
***And the fish took him below.***

***"In my distress I called to the Lord, and He answered me. From the depths of the grave I called for help, and You listened to my cry."***

***2:2***

# *MICAH*

***The word of the Lord came down to Micah,***
***His anger against Judah was very clear.***
***The people did wrong in the sight of God,***
***The day of judgement was very near.***

***"He has shown you, O man, what is good. And what does the Lord require of you? To act justly, and to love mercy, and to walk humbly with your God."***

***6:8***

# *NAHUM*

***Nahum assures the people of Judah***
***The city of Nineveh God will destroy.***
***He protects His people from their enemies,***
***When you obey Him, He gives you joy.***

***"The Lord is good, a refuge in times of trouble. He cares for those who trust in Him."***

***1:7***

# *HABAKKUK*

***Habakkuk teaches us a lesson***
***That God punishes those who sin.***
***The injustice and violence in Judah***
***Brought the people to a painful end.***

***"Your eyes are too pure to look on evil;***
***You cannot tolerate wrong."***

***1:13***

# ***ZEPHANIAH***

***The people of Judah continued to sin,***
***So Zephaniah comes on the scene.***
***He preached to the people to return to God,***
***And told of God's judgement he had forseen.***

***"Seek the Lord, all you humble of the land, you who do what He commands. Seek righteousness, seek humility, perhaps you will be sheltered on the day of the Lord's anger."***

***2:3***

# ***HAGGAI***

***Haggai preached to the people of Judah***
***That God's temple must be rebuilt.***
***Deny yourself, and put God first,***
***Or you'll be punished for your guilt.***

***"...Be strong, all you people of the land, declares the Lord, and work. For I am with you, declares the Lord Almighty."***

***2:4***

# *ZECHARIAH*

***Return to the Lord, and He'll return to you,***
***Zechariah continued to preach,***
***Build God's temple, and obey His Word,***
***And His blessings will be in your reach.***

***"This is what the Lord Almighty says: If you will walk in my ways and keep my requirements, then you will govern my house and have charge of my courts, and I will give you a place among these standing there."***

***3:7***

# *MALACHI*

***The last book of the Old Testament***
***Tells us that God wants our best;***
***Our gifts, obedience, and our love***
***Will decide if we pass the test.***

***"A son honors his father, and a servant his master. If I am a Father, where is the honor due me? If I am a Master, where is the respect due me? Says the Lord Almighty."***

***1:6***

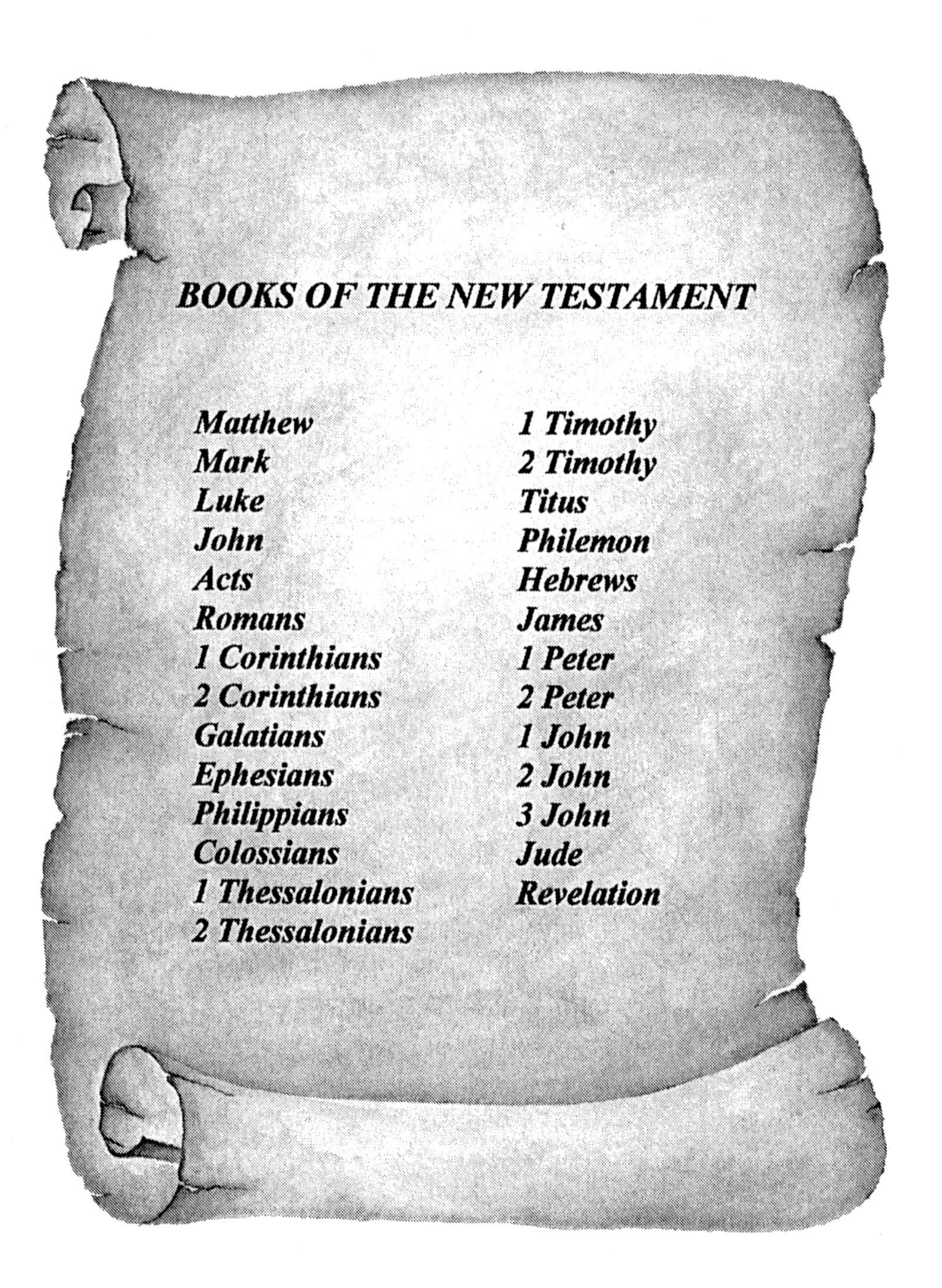

## *BOOKS OF THE NEW TESTAMENT*

*Matthew*
*Mark*
*Luke*
*John*
*Acts*
*Romans*
*1 Corinthians*
*2 Corinthians*
*Galatians*
*Ephesians*
*Philippians*
*Colossians*
*1 Thessalonians*
*2 Thessalonians*
*1 Timothy*
*2 Timothy*
*Titus*
*Philemon*
*Hebrews*
*James*
*1 Peter*
*2 Peter*
*1 John*
*2 John*
*3 John*
*Jude*
*Revelation*

# *INTRODUCTION TO THE NEW TESTAMENT*

***The New Testament, the second part of the Christian Bible, contains 27 books. It is a record of the promises made by God to man, and shows the teachings and experiences of Jesus Christ and his followers.***

***The New Testament teaches us about Jesus' birth, death, and resurrection. It explains how the Christian church began, its struggles, and tells about the many followers of Jesus Christ who helped it to grow.***

# *MATTHEW*

***Matthew was one of the twelve disciples.***
***He tells about Jesus from the manger to the cross.***
***We learn about the parables and miracles of Jesus.***
***Without these teaching, many souls will be lost.***

***"Jesus replied: Love the Lord your God with all your heart and with all your soul and with all your mind.***
***This is the first and greatest commandment.***
***And the second is like it. Love your neighbor as yourself."***

***22: 37-39***

# ***MARK***

***Mark recorded the story of Jesus***
***To help the Romans to understand***
***That Jesus Christ is the Son of God,***
***Who was sent to earth to fulfill God's plan.***

***"For even the Son of Man did not come to be served, but to serve, and to give His life as a ransom for many."***

***10:45***

# *LUKE*

***Luke, a physician, and a friend of Paul,***
***Wrote this account of Jesus for all to see.***
***He tells of His life and death on the cross,***
***Where He died to save humanity.***

***"He was a prophet, powerful in word and deed before God and all the people."***

***24:19***

# ***JOHN***

***John, the disciple that Jesus loved,***
***Wrote about Christ's early ministry.***
***He helped us understand who Jesus is,***
***And the events that took Him to Calvary.***

***"For God so loved the world that He gave His only Son, that whosoever believes in Him shall not perish but have everlasting life."***

***3:16***

# *ACTS*

***Luke writes about the struggle of the early church.***
***He tells about the heroes who helped it grow.***
***We learn about Saul, who God changed to Paul.***
***Then he preached about Jesus so all would know.***

***"But you will receive power when the Holy Spirit comes on you; and you will be my witness in Jerusalem, and in all Judea and Samaria, and to the ends of the earth."***

***1:8***

# ***ROMANS***

***Paul wrote this letter to the church in Rome***
***To inform them of God's righteousness.***
***He gives us a blueprint of how to live.***
***If we follow his teachings, God surely will bless.***

***"This righteousness from God comes through faith in Jesus Christ to all who believe…"***

***3:23***

# *1 CORINTHIANS*

***The church in Corinth had problems,***
***So Paul wrote this letter to explain***
***That Jesus gave rules for His church***
***Which His people are required to maintain.***

***"I appeal to you, brothers, in the name of our Lord Jesus Christ, that all of you agree with one another so that there may be no divisions among you, and that you may be perfectly united in mind and thought."***

***1:10***

# *2 CORINTHIANS*

***Paul opens his hearts to the Corinthians.***
***He gives them advice from God above.***
***He rejoices in their victories,***
***And he reminds them of his love.***

***"You show that you are a letter from Christ... written not with ink, but with the Spirit of the living God, not on tablets of stone, but on tablets of human hearts."***

***3:3***

# ***GALATIANS***

***The church in Galatia was confused***
***About which law they ought to live by.***
***So Paul wrote this letter to them***
***In an effort to clarify.***

***"I do not set aside the grace of God, for if righteousness could be gained through the law, Christ died for nothing."***

***2:21***

# *EPHESIANS*

***While in prison, Paul wrote to the Ephesians***
***To help them to understand***
***That the church is not in a building,***
***But in our hearts, our minds, and our hands.***

***"For we are God's workmanship, created in Christ Jesus to do good works, which God prepared in advance for us to do."***

***2:10***

# *PHILIPPIANS*

***The Philippians continued to obey God,***
***Even though Paul was still away.***
***He praised them for their faithfulness,***
***And encouraged them not to go astray.***

***"Do not be anxious about anything, but in everything, by prayer and petition with thanksgiving, present your requests to God."***

***4:6***

# ***COLOSSIANS***

***The Colossians believed Christ was supreme.***
***Their faith and love kept them from wrong.***
***While still in chains, Paul wrote to them,***
***And prayed to God to keep them strong.***

***"Let the word of Christ dwell in you richly as you teach and admonish one another with all wisdom, as you sing psalms, hymns and spiritual songs with gratitude in your hearts to God."***

***3:16***

# *1 THESSALONIANS*

***The Thessalonians were new Christians.***
***Paul wrote this letter of encouragement.***
***They turned their backs on idol gods,***
***To worship the God who is omnipotent.***

***"For God did not call us to be impure, but to live a holy life."***

***4:7***

# *2 THESSALONIANS*

***The Thessalonians were persecuted***
***Because they loved God and tried to live right.***
***Paul's letter was to encourage them***
***To stand firm and continue to fight.***

***"May our Lord Jesus Christ…encourage your hearts and strengthen you in every good deed and work."***

***2:16-1***

# *1 TIMOTHY*

***Timothy, a young helper and friend of Paul,***
***Tried to teach the Christians how to live.***
***He taught them the rules for God's church,***
***And how to love each other and freely give.***

***"Don't let anyone look down on you because you are young, but set an example for the believers in speech, in life, in love, in faith, and in purity."***

***4:12***

# *2 TIMOTHY*

***Paul was taken back to prison,***
***He soon was deserted by his friends.***
***He appealed to Timothy to continue to teach,***
***And don't be ashamed of God before other men.***

***"Do your best to present yourself to God as one approved, a workman who does not need to be ashamed, and who correctly handles the word of truth."***

***2:15***

# *TITUS*

***Paul explains in this letter to Titus***
***How to be a good leader and teacher:***
***Teach the old, the young, the women and men***
***To obey God and to honor the preacher.***

***"Remind the people … to be obedient and be ready to do whatever is good."***

***3:1***

# *PHILEMON*

***In this short letter to Philemon***
***Paul makes a strong appeal,***
***That he accepts Onesimus, the runaway slave,***
***Who served Paul with great zeal.***

***"I pray that you may be active in sharing your faith, so that you will have a full understanding of every good thing we have in Christ."***

***6***

# *HEBREWS*

***Hebrews affirms Jesus as our High Priest,***
***Who intercedes for us to God on high.***
***It tells about Moses and Melchizedek,***
***And the heroes of faith who we glorify.***

***"For we do not have a high priest who is unable to sympathize with our weaknesses, but we have one who has been tempted in every way, just as we are - yet was without sin."***

***4:15***

# *JAMES*

***James, God's servant and brother of Jesus,***
***Gave us directions for Christian living.***
***He taught about faith and the deeds we do.***
***If we pray and believe, God will keep on giving.***

***"...The prayer of a righteous man is powerful and effective."***

***5:16***

# *1 PETER*

***Peter wrote this letter of encouragement***
***To suffering Christians everywhere.***
***He said to be holy and submit to God,***
***And He will hear you and answer your prayer.***

***"But you are a chosen people, a royal priesthood, a holy nation, a people belonging to God, that you may declare the praises of Him who called you out of darkness into His wonderful light."***

***2:9***

# ***2 PETER***

***Peter warns the Christians against false teachers,
Who will change and distort God's word.
He tells them to get goodness and knowledge,
And live by the Scriptures they've heard.***

***"But grow in grace and knowledge of our Lord and Savior Jesus Christ. To Him be glory both now and forever."***

***3:18***

# *1 JOHN*

***John says to love God, and walk in the light.***
***Don't love the world and the things therein.***
***Love your brother and do what God commands.***
***Resist the Antichrist who cause you to sin.***

***"...If we walk in the light, as He is in the light, we have fellowship with one another, and the blood of Jesus, His Son, purifies us from all sin."***

***1:7***

# *2 JOHN*

***To be close to God, you must abide in His word,***
***And be obedient to our Father above.***
***You must walk in the truth that lives in you,***
***Avoid deceivers, and treat others with love.***

***"And this is love: that we walk in obedience to His commands. As you have heard from the beginning, His command is that you walk in love."***

***6***

# ***3 JOHN***

***John wrote to Gaius, a dear friend***
***To praise him for his faithfulness.***
***He showed love to strangers who came to the church***
***If we follow his example, God surely will bless.***

***"Dear friend, do not imitate what is evil, but what is good. Anyone who does what is good is from God…"***

***11***

# ***JUDE***

***Jude, the brother of James and Jesus,***
***Warns the Christians of godless men.***
***He encourages them to pray in the spirit,***
***And to keep their brothers from yielding to sin.***

***"Keep yourselves in God's love as you wait for the mercy of our Lord Jesus Christ to bring you to eternal life."***

***21***

# ***REVELATION***

***John had a vision of things to come.***
***He wrote them down for all Christians to see***
***That God alone will judge the world,***
***And Jesus will have the final victory.***

***"...Hallelujah! For our Lord God Almighty reigns.***
***Let us rejoice and be glad and give Him glory."***

***19:6-7***

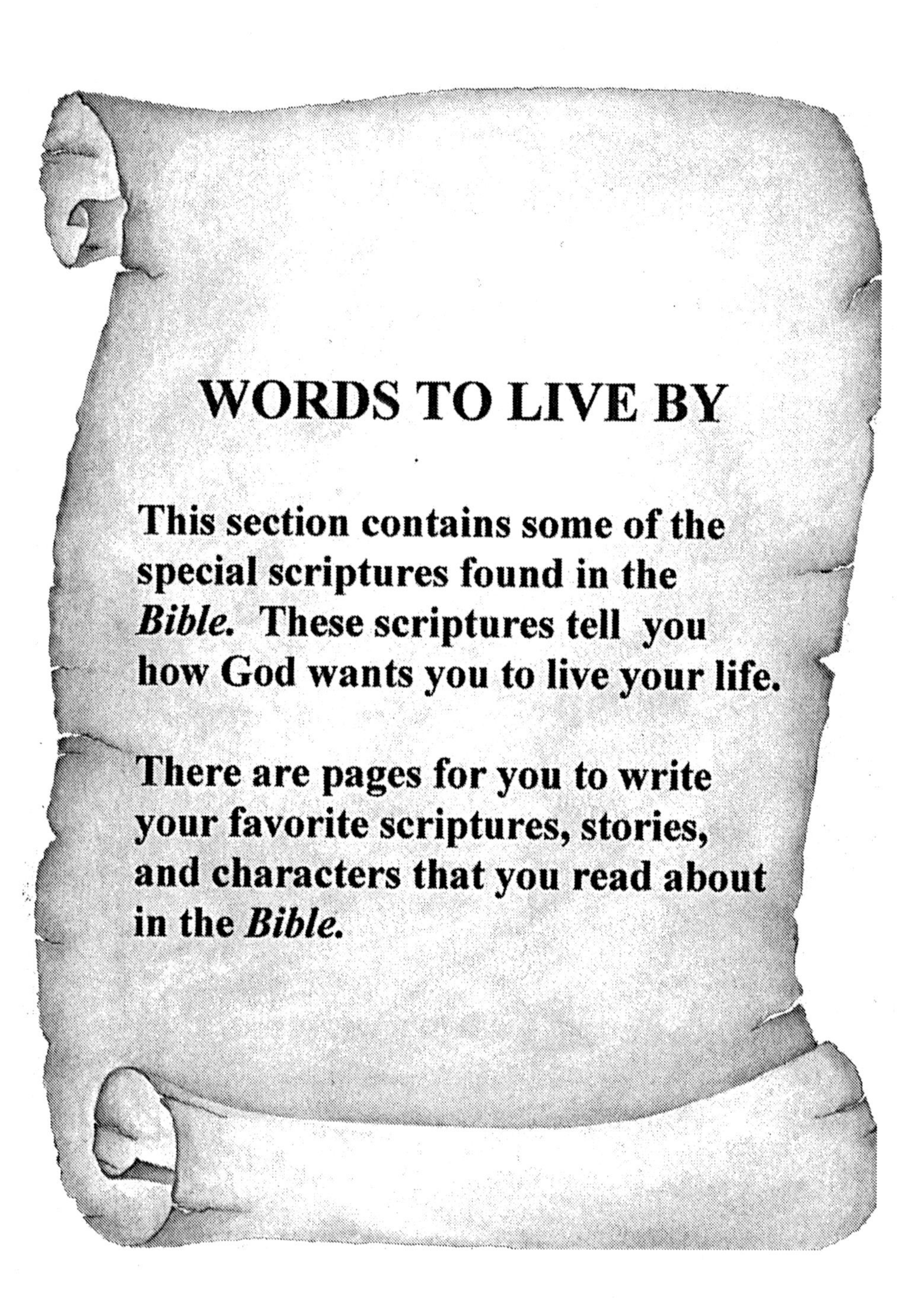

# WORDS TO LIVE BY

**This section contains some of the special scriptures found in the *Bible.* These scriptures tell you how God wants you to live your life.**

**There are pages for you to write your favorite scriptures, stories, and characters that you read about in the *Bible.***

# ABCs OF WISDOM FROM PROVERBS

**A**ll a man's ways seem right to him, but the Lord weighs the heart.

21:2

**B**lessed is the man who always fears the Lord, but he who hardens his heart falls into trouble.

28:14

**C**ommit to the Lord whatever you do, and your plans will succeed.

16:3

**D**o not make friends with a hot-tempered man, do not associate with one easily angered.

22:24

**E**ven a child is known by his actions, by whether his conduct is pure and right.

20:11

**F**or whoever finds Me finds life and receives favor from the Lord.

8:35

**G**old there is, and rubies in abundance, but lips that speak knowledge are a rare jewel.

20:15

**H**old on to instruction, do not let it go; guard it well, for it is your life.

4:13

**I** love those who love me, and those who seek me find me.

8:17

When **J**ustice is done, it brings joy to the righteous but terror to evildoers.

21:15

**K**eep my commandments and you will live; guard my teachings as the apple of your eye.

7:2

Laziness brings on deep sleep, and the shiftless man goes hungry.

19:15

Misfortune pursues the sinner, but prosperity is the reward of the righteous.

13:21

Now then, my sons, listen to me; blessed are those who keep my ways.

8:32

One man gives freely, yet gains even more; another withholds unduly, but comes to poverty.

11:24

Pride only breeds quarrels, but wisdom is found in those who take advice.

13:10

A Quick-tempered man does foolish things, and a crafty man is hated.

14:17

**R**ich and poor have this in common:
The Lord is the Maker of them all.

22:2

**S**eldom set foot in your neighbor's house- too much of you, and he will hate you.

25:17

**T**he fear of the Lord is the beginning of knowledge, but fools despise wisdom and discipline.

1:7

**U**nderstanding is the fountain of life to those who have it, but folly brings punishment to fools.

16:22

Do not envy a **V**iolent man or choose any of his ways.

3:31

**W**ise men store up knowledge, but the mouth of a fool invites ruin.

10:14

**X** (Don't X out anything that God has said.) B.J.G.

**Y**ou who are simple, gain prudence; you who are foolish, gain understanding.

8:5

It is not good to have **Z**eal without knowledge, nor to be hasty and miss the way.

19:2

# THE TEN COMMANDMENTS

**Exodus 20: 2-17**
**Deuteronomy 5: 6-21**

1. **You shall have no other gods before Me.**
2. **You shall not make for yourself an idol in the form of anything in heaven above or on the earth beneath or in the waters below.**
3. **You shall not misuse the name of the Lord your God, for the Lord will not hold anyone guiltless who misuses His name.**
4. **Observe the Sabbath day by keeping it holy as the Lord your God has commanded you.**
5. **Honor your father and your mother, as the Lord your God has commanded you, so that you may live long and that it may go well with you in the land the Lord your God is giving you.**
6. **You shall not murder.**
7. **You shall not commit adultery.**
8. **You shall not steal**
9. **You shall not give false testimony against your neighbor.**
10. **You shall not covet your neighbor's wife. You shall not set your desire on your neighbor's house or land, his manservant or maidservant, his ox or donkey, or anything that belongs to your neighbor.**

# THE LORD'S PRAYER

**Matthew 6: 9-13**

Our Father which are in heaven.
Hallowed by thy name,
thy kingdom come,
thy will be done on earth
as it is in heaven.
Give us this day our daily bread,
and forgive our debts
as we forgive our debtors.
And lead us not into temptation,
but deliver us from evil.
For thine is the kingdom,
and the power,
and the glory.
Forever and ever.

Amen

# *PRAYER OF JABEZ*

**Oh, that you would**
**bless me indeed, and**
**enlarge my territory,**
**that your hand would**
**be with me, and that**
**You would keep**
**me from evil,**
**that I may not**
**cause pain.**

**1Chronicles 4:10**

# THE BEATITUDES

## Matthew 5: 1-12

**His (Jesus') disciples came to him, and he began to teach them, saying:**

**Blessed are the poor in spirit,**
**For theirs is the kingdom of heaven.**

**Blessed are those who mourn,**
**For they will be comforted.**

**Blessed are the meek,**
**For they will inherit the earth.**

**Blessed are those who hunger and thirst for righteousness,**
**For they will be filled.**

**Blessed are the merciful,**
**For they will be shown mercy.**

**Blessed are the pure in heart,**
**For they shall see God.**

**Blessed are the peacemakers,**
**For they will be called sons of God.**

**Blessed are those who are persecuted because of righteousness,**
**For theirs is the kingdom of heaven.**

**Blessed are you when people insult you, persecute you and falsely say all kinds of evil against you because of me.**

**Rejoice and be glad, because great is your reward in heaven,**

**For in the same way they persecuted the prophets who were before me.**

# PSALM 23

The Lord is my shepherd,
I shall not want.
He makes me lie down in green pastures,
He leads me beside the still waters,
He restores my soul.
He leads me in the path of righteousness
for his name's sake.
Yea, though I walk through the valley
of the shadow of death,
I will fear no evil, for Thou are with me.
Thy rod and thy staff, they comfort me.
Thou prepare a table before me
in the presence of my enemies.
Thou anoint my head with oil,
my cup runs over.
Surely goodness and mercy shall follow me, all the
days of my life.
And I shall dwell in the house of the Lord forever.

# THE FRUIT OF THE SPIRIT

Galatians 5:22-23

But the fruit of the Spirit is love, joy, peace, patience, kindness, goodness, gentleness, and self-control. Against such things there is no law.

## **Who is the greatest in the kingdom of heaven?** (Matthew 18: 1-4)

At that time the disciples came to Jesus and asked, "Who is the greatest in the kingdom of heaven?"

He called a little child and had him stand among them.

And he said: "I tell you the truth, unless you change and become like little children, you will never enter the kingdom of heaven.

Therefore, whoever humbles himself like this child is the greatest in the kingdom of heaven.

**God wants us all to be like little children.**

# *SPREADING THE GOOD NEWS*

## *By Bernice Jackson Graham*

***On his way to Damascus,***
***Saul was blinded by a flash of light.***
***Then God spoke to him***
***And commanded that he stop his fight.***

***The story continues, as you well know,***
***That Saul was changed to Paul.***
***He went about preaching the word of God,***
***On his new mission he stood tall.***

***Paul preached and healed in the name of God.***
***For himself he wanted no fame.***
***Even though he was thrown into jail,***
***He still preached Jesus' name.***

***How many of us can be like Paul,***
***Spreading the Good News along our way?***
***We seem to be ever so speechless***
***When there is so much we can say.***

***We kneel down and we pray to God,***
***And His blessings we receive,***
***But we fail to tell the unsaved soul***
***To help him to believe.***

***God has been so good to us.***
***He gave His only son.***
***The least we can do is tell others***
***Of the goodness He has done.***

***Spreading the Good News is our mission.***
***It isn't so hard to do.***
***You must go out and tell the story.***
***Maybe someone is waiting for you.***

# MY FAVORITE SCRIPTURES

# MY FAVORITE BIBLE STORIES

# MY FAVORITE BIBLE CHARACTERS

Printed in the United States
964900001B